Ready, Set, Kindergarten!

Paula Ayer

Art by **Danielle Arbour**

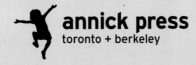

annick press
toronto + berkeley

Cover art/design by Danielle Arbour
Edited by Debbie Rogosin
Designed by Danielle Arbour

Annick Press Ltd.

We acknowledge the support of the Canada Council for the Arts, the Ontario Arts Council, and the participation of the Government of Canada/la participation du gouvernement du Canada for our publishing activities.

Cataloging in Publication

Ayer, Paula, author
        Ready, set, kindergarten! / Paula Ayer ; Danielle Arbour, illustrator.

Issued in print and electronic formats.
        ISBN 978-1-55451-704-6 (bound).--ISBN 978-1-55451-703-9 (pbk.).--
        ISBN 978-1-55451-706-0 (pdf).--ISBN 978-1-55451-705-3 (epub)

        I. Arbour, Danielle, 1967-, illustrator II. Title.

PS8601.Y39R43 2015   jC813'.6   C2014-904511-5
                                              C2014-904512-3

Published in the U.S.A. by Annick Press (U.S.) Ltd.
Distributed in Canada by University of Toronto Press.
Distributed in the U.S.A. by Publishers Group West.

Printed in Canada

Visit us at: www.annickpress.com
Visit Danielle Arbour at: www.daniellearbour.com

Also available in e-book format.
Please visit www.annickpress.com/ebooks.html for more details.

For Sulekha — P.A.
To my sweet children, Liam and Ava
— D.A.

Whoosh on my jacket.

Smoosh on my shoes.

Dressing myself.
I'm getting ready!

Looking at signs.

Calling out **letters**.

 Finding some **words**. I'm ready to learn.

Painting a picture.

Cutting out shapes.

Building **strong fingers**.

I'm ready to work.

Jumping and twirling
and reaching up high!

Stretching my body.

I'm ready to move.

Baking a **cake** with a bucket and sand.

Having fun on my own.

I'm ready to **imagine**.

Splashing with **water**.

Scrubbing with **soap**.

Washing my hands.

I'm ready to **eat**!

Playing with **friends**.
Hey, that's *my* toy!

Sharing is hard.

I'm not always ready.

Making my stuffies
have a **BIG FIGHT**.

Saying I'm sorry...
I'm ready to try.

Setting the table.
Counting out plates.

1

2

3

4

5

Needing some **help**.

I'm ready to ask.

Jumping into my **jammies**.

Brushing my **teeth**.

Hugs and kisses **goodnight**.

Now I'm ready to sleep.

Toasting some bread.
Pouring some milk.

Filling my tummy. I'm ready to leave.

Going to school. Waving good-bye.

I'm starting **kindergarten**—

and I think I'm **ready**!